THE EROTIC SENTIMENT

In the Paintings of India and Nepal

Once the Wheel of Love has been set in motion, there is no absolute rule.
Kama Sutra

The Erotic Sentiment

In the
Paintings of India and Nepal

Nik Douglas and

Penny Slinger

Park Street Press
R O C H E S T E R • V E R M O N T

Park Street Press
One Park Street
Rochester, Vermont   05767

Library of Congress Cataloging-in-Publication Data
Douglas, Nik.
The erotic sentiment : in the paintings of India & Nepal : pillow book /
by Nik Douglas & Penny Slinger.
p.   cm.
Rev. ed. of: The pillow book. c1981.
ISBN 0-89281-208-7 (v. 1)
1. Erotic painting, India.   2. Miniature painting, India.   3. Erotic painting, Nepali.
I. Slinger, Penny, 1947–   .   II. Douglas, Nik.   Pillow book.   III. Title.
ND1337.I5D68   1988
88-30887
757'.8'0954—dc19
CIP

Printed and bound in Italy

1 3 5 7 9 8 6 4 2

Park Street Press is a division of Inner Traditions International, Ltd.
Distributed to the book trade in the United States by Harper and Row Publishers, Inc.
Distributed to the book trade in Canada by Book Center, Inc., Montreal, Quebec

CONTENTS

LIST OF COLOR PLATES

15 Gouache on heavy paper, Kathmandu Sirohi-style, Nepal, c. 1830, size: 41 × 49.8 cm. **16** Gouache on paper, East India Company school, c. 1880, size: 20.6 × 25.6 cm. **17** Gouache on paper, Rajasthan, c. 1800, size: 15 × 21.1 cm. **18** Gouache on paper, East India Company school, India, c. 1880, size: 20.5 × 25.5 cm. **19** Gouache on paper, East India Company school, c. 1880, size: 20.4 × 25.5 cm. **20** Gouache on heavy paper, Kathmandu Sirohi-style, Nepal, c. 1830, size: 40.6 × 51 cm. **21** Gouache on heavy paper, Kathmandu Sirohi-style, Nepal, c. 1830, size: 40.6 × 49.8 cm. **22** Gouache on heavy paper, Kathmandu Sirohi-style, Nepal, c. 1830, size: 40.2 × 50.5 cm. **23** Gouache on paper, Rajasthan Hills, India, c. 1800, size: 14.7 × 23.3 cm. **24** Gouache on paper, Rajasthan Bundi-style, India, c. 1800, size: 13.2 × 21 cm. **25** Gouache on paper, Rajasthan Hills Sirohi-style, India, c. 1800, size: 16.2 × 23.8 cm. **26** Gouache on paper, Jodhpur school, India, dated 1830, size: 23.5 × 32 cm. **27** Watercolor on paper, East India Company school, c. 1900, size: 10.5 × 12.7 cm. **28** Gouache on heavy paper, Kathmandu Sirohi-style, Nepal, c. 1830, size: 42.7 × 50.5 cm. **29** Gouache on heavy paper, Kathmandu Sirohi-style, Nepal, c. 1830, size: 39.8 × 49 cm. **30** Gouache on heavy paper, Kathmandu Sirohi-style, Nepal, c. 1830, size: 40.9 × 49 cm. **31** Gouache on heavy paper, Kathmandu Sirohi-style, Nepal, c. 1830, size: 41.3 × 48.5 cm. **32** Gouache on paper, Jodhpur, India, dated 1830, size: 23 × 31.2 cm. **33** Gouache on paper, Jodhpur school, India, dated 1830, size: 24 × 29.2 cm. **34** Watercolor on paper, Rajasthan, mid-19th century, size: 14 × 21 cm. **35** Gouache on paper, Rajasthan Hills, India, mid-18th century, size: 22 × 27.8 cm. **36** Gouache on paper, Rajasthan Hills Sirohi-style, India, c. 1800, size: 20.5 × 28 cm. **37** Gouache on paper, Rajasthan Hills Sirohi-style, India, c. 1800, size: 15.9 × 23.8 cm. **38** Gouache on heavy paper, Kathmandu Sirohi-style, Nepal, c. 1830, size: 39 × 47.2 cm. **39** Gouache on heavy paper, Kathmandu Sirohi-style, Nepal, c. 1830, size: 38.4 × 48.8 cm. **40** Gouache on paper, Rajasthan Hills Sirohi-style, India, c. 1800, size: 20.4 × 28.1 cm. **41** Gouache on paper, Rajasthan Bundi-style, India, late 18th century, size: 13.7 × 20 cm. **42** Gouache on paper, Rajasthan Hills Sirohi-style, India, c. 1800, size: 20.5 × 28.2 cm. **43** Gouache on paper, Jodhpur, India, dated 1830, size: 22.9 × 31.2 cm. **44** Gouache on paper, Bundi school, India, c. 1800, size: 20.4 × 24.8 cm. **45** Gouache on paper, Rajasthan Hills Sirohi-style, India, c. 1800, size: 20.5 × 28.2 cm. **46** Watercolor on paper, East India Company school, c. 1900, size: 10.5 × 12.7 cm. **47** Gouache on paper, Rajasthan Hills Sirohi-style, India, c. 1800, size: 20.4 × 28.2 cm. **48** Gouache on paper, East India Company school, India, c. 1900, size: 9.9 × 12.6 cm. **49** Gouache on paper, East India Company school, India, c. 1900, size: 24.5 × 29 cm. **50** Gouache on paper, Rajasthan Hills, India, c. 1800, size: 14.7 × 23.3 cm. **51** Gouache on paper, Rajasthan Sirohi-style, India, c. 1800, size: 16.5 × 20.7 cm. **52** Gouache on paper, Rajasthan, c. 1900, size: 23.4 × 32.7 cm. **53** Watercolor on paper, Bengal, India, early 18th century, size: 18.4 × 26.9 cm. **54** Gouache on paper, Rajasthan Hills Sirohi-style, India, c. 1800, size: 20.5 × 28 cm. **55** Gouache on paper, Rajasthan Hills Sirohi-style, India, c. 1800, size: 20.5 × 28 cm. **56** Gouache on heavy paper, Kathmandu Sirohi-style, Nepal, c. 1830, size: 42.1 × 46.5 cm. **57** Gouache on paper, Rajasthan Bundi-style, India, late 18th century, size: 13.3 × 19.7 cm. **58** Gouache on paper, Rajasthan Hills Sirohi-style, India, c. 1800, size: 20.6 × 28.1 cm. **59** Watercolor on paper, Bengal, India, early 18th century, size: 18.3 × 26.9 cm. **60** Watercolor on paper, Bengal, India, early 18th century, size: 19 × 27 cm. **61** Watercolor on paper, Bengal, India, early 18th century, size: 18.5 × 26.9 cm. **62** Watercolor on paper, with gold applied, Deccan Mughal style, India, c. 1700, size: 12.2 × 18.7 cm. **63** Watercolor on paper, with gold applied, Deccan Mughal style, India, c. 1700, size: 12.2 × 18.7 cm. **64** Gouache on paper, Rajasthan, India, c. 1880, size: 15 × 22.8 cm. **65** Gouache on paper, Rajasthan Rajput, India, c. 1800, size: 25 × 34.4 cm. **66** Gouache on heavy paper, Kathmandu Sirohi-style, Nepal, c. 1830, size: 39.4 × 47.8 cm. **67** Gouache on paper, Rajasthan Bundi-style, India late 18th century, size: 19.3 × 12.6 cm. **68** Gouache on paper, Bundi school, India, c. 1800, size: 19.6 × 26.8 cm. **69** Gouache on paper, Bundi school, India, c. 1800, size: 20.5 × 26.7 cm. **70** Gouache on paper, Jodhpur school, India, dated 1830, size: 29 × 34.2 cm. **71** Gouache on paper, Jodhpur school, India, dated 1830, size: 23 × 31.4 cm. **72** Gouache on paper, Basohli school, India, early 18th century, size: 10.2 × 14.8 cm. **73** Gouache on paper, Lucknow school, India, c. 1900, size: 21.2 × 28.1 cm. **74** Gouache on paper, Rajasthan, India, late 18th century, size: 12.9 × 15.4 cm. **75** Gouache on paper, Jaipur Rajasthan school, India, c. 1800, size: 18 × 24.4 cm. **76** Gouache on paper, Rajasthan, India, c. 1800, size: 20.4 × 25.5 cm. **77** Gouache on paper, Rajasthan, India, early 19th century, size: 24.6 × 31 cm. **78** Gouache on paper, Jodhpur school, India, c. 1780, size: 12.6 × 19.7 cm. **79** Gouache on heavy paper, Kathmandu Sirohi-style, Nepal, c. 1830, size: 39 × 49 cm.

THE EROTIC SENTIMENT

In Hindu Culture and Painting

The erotic sentiment arises in connection with favorable seasons, garlands, ornaments, enjoying the company of beloved ones, music, and poetry, and going to the garden and roaming there.

Bharata

The erotic sentiment is a significant ingredient of Hindu culture. It colors religious ceremonies, ritual procedures, devotional songs, classic poetry, drama, music, dance, sculpture, painting and most of the other fine arts of ancient India. During India's Vedic period (c. 1200–800 B.C.) sacred hymns evoked the erotic sentiment to describe feelings of mystic ecstasy and oneness with the Divine.

In a society where sex was openly cultivated as a worthy art form, it is not surprising that the erotic sentiment was studied and cultivated to a very high level of refinement. Indian art in particular has always been much influenced by the erotic sentiment. The suggestive smile of the courtesan, the evocative symbolism of the poet, the subtle tones of the musician, the graceful movements of the dancer, the curvaceous forms of the sculptor, the rich colors and enchanting symbolism of the painter all were carefully contrived expressions of the erotic sentiment. Any thorough study of Indian art must be based on a complete understanding of the significance and role of the erotic sentiment in traditional Hindu culture.

Depictions of erotic themes are to be found among archaeological material derived from the great Indus Valley civilization, done on clay moldings, stone seals, pottery, clay or stone figurines, and in some cave paintings done during the period 1500 to 500 B.C. The connection between erotic coupling and fertility had no doubt been established in ancient times, and cults emerged which elevated the sexual act to a religious duty. Most of the erotic art of the early period is connected to fertility cults, with the glorification of the mother goddess being a very popular theme. Depictions of the sexual organs, in abstract or realistic style, are among material excavated from the Indus Valley sites of Mohenjo Daro and Harappa. There are also figures seated in yoga postures, often accompanied by bulls or horn emblems, as well as representations of plants sprouting from the sexual organs of goddesses of different types, and fine bronze castings of dancing girls posing sensuously.

Many of the Vedic texts refer to ritualistic lovemaking, symbolic pairing or "coupling" of ceremonial ingredients, obscene dialogues in religious context, and the acquisition of magical powers or "boons" through the practice of sexual disciplines. It was believed that the generative powers of nature could be stimulated and directed by following precise sexual practices which were considered to be highly potent and auspicious. Fertility festivals in ancient India were times of gaiety and free sexual license, ranging from ritual love-making, dancing, the telling of obscene stories, erotic mimicry, wild orgies, and organized gatherings of courtesans. These fertility festivals were considered necessary and extremely lucky.

Terracottas showing couples in sexual union were quite common in northern India from 200 B.C. to 300 A.D., and numerous examples have survived. During this phase some erotic stone sculpture was made, showing couples in various stages of sexual union. Known as *Maithunas* or "unions," they were used to decorate temples and were believed to be auspicious and protective from the forces of evil. In fact, depictions of couples in love dalliance were always viewed by Indians as "lucky" themes. For example, several of the paintings of multiple lovemaking in complex horse shapes, done in the later period, are purely talismanic and were created with the purpose of attracting good fortune through the magical power of sex.

Many Buddhist monuments of the early period were decorated with *Maithunas* and sculptures of scantily clad, heavenly nymphs. Later, such erotic subjects became even more common, with whole temple facades covered with finely carved sensuous scenes, often depicting lovers in a multitude of erotic positions.

The Tantric influence, which developed in full between the eighth and twelfth centuries A.D., caused both Hindu and Buddhist culture to take up erotic themes in a more organized and meaningful way. This Tantric tradition, both Hindu and Buddhist, emphasized the natural interrelationship of microcosm and macrocosm, the "inner" and "outer" realities, developing an evolved sexual-yogic technology which focused on love postures, breath control, the repetition of power syllables and phrases (*mantras*), and visualizations. These intentional, practical, or ritual acts, all done in an ordered way, were the foundation of Tantric practice and were conceived of as a "weaving together" of the objective and sub-jective aspects of individual reality, as a means to overcome the endless cycle of rebirth. The Tantric tradition explored and developed precise techniques for channeling and transforming sexual energy into the bliss of Liberation. Art forms emerged as expressions of this ideal. The great temple complexes at Khajuraho and Konarak were visual celebrations of the erotic sentiment, with many of the compositions charged with mystic meaning, which can be interpreted according to Tantric philosophy. As erotic painting and sculpture emerged as lasting expressions of mystic couplings "charged" with magical power, all forms of sexual expression were shown.

Hinduism defines four principle objects of life, these being "religious and social duty" (*Dharma*), "the acquisition of wealth" (*Artha*), "the pursuit of sensual pleasure" (*Kama*) and "the attainment of spiritual liberation" (*Moksha*). The Sanskrit term *Kama*, generally translated as "love," means the enjoyment of all the five normal senses—sight, smell, taste, touch, and hearing, plus a sixth "sense," the mind. Perfection in the art of love requires a balanced combination of these six ingredients. No other art is so demanding or fulfilling.

All Indian culture is said to be of divine origin and the Hindu art of love is no exception. Thus, it was Brahma the Creator who first codified the literature of love and it was the very virile Nandi, the bull of Shiva (the Transcendental, the Supreme Yogi) who abridged it into a form suitable for the sages, who in turn simplified it for mortals. The erotic or "love" sentiment soon became regarded as the first and most important among the nine classically recognized sentiments, the others being the humorous, heroic, marvelous, peaceful, pitiful, furious, disgusting, and terrific. Of these nine sentiments, the first five were considered to be of a blissful nature, and the last four of a painful nature. Traditionally each sentiment is ruled by a deity and is considered to be a personification of a particular color and tone. The erotic sentiment is linked to the deity Vishnu, "The Preserver," and to the dark blue or black color.

The *Kama Sutra*, a comprehensive treatise on sex and love, was written down by the inspired sage Vatsyayana in the late second century A.D. This was a time when courtesans occupied an important and respected position in a lavish society. Cities were famous for their monuments, gardens and expecially for their courtesans, who usually were highly skilled singers and dancers, sometimes referred to as "Mistresses of the Sixty-four Arts," of which the art of love was considered foremost.

Courtesans were part of a king's retinue, or were attached to the palaces of princes, and were set up in pleasure houses patronized by the wealthy. They were generally considered to be among the assets of any great city. Courtesans were also great patrons of all the arts; it was said that courtesans were the real rulers of high society, creating fashions and fads, promoting the sixty-four arts (music, dancing, painting, decoration, flower-arranging, cosmetics, perfumery, cooking, acting, animal and bird training, massage, dressing, horticulture, and so forth) and guiding their patrons through their great specialty, the science and art of love. On occasions courtesans were presented as gifts to distinguished visitors or to returning heroes. One thing we can be sure of is that courtesans were considered to be embodiments of the erotic sentiment and as such were virtually worshipped as goddesses.

Art galleries (*Chitra Salas*) and theaters were included among places of culture patronized by courtesans and their clients. Many art galleries and theaters of ancient India are known to have held exhibitions of erotic subjects, some of which are likely to have been portraits of famous courtesans in different intimate positions of union with their most celebrated clients. Since we know that no stigma was attached to a person visiting courtesans, and that it was even customary for husband and wife to appear in public accompanied by favored courtesans, we can assume that renderings of erotic scenes were well received. The *Natya Shastra*, a classical Hindu text on the art of dance, written in the second century A.D., describes theater halls "decorated with amorous paintings and bedecked with sculptures of languorous lovelies."

Dramatic entertainment in ancient India was conceived of as an assemblage or "collage" of sentiments. Used in the same way that a painter combines the colors on the palette, different combinations of sentiments created different hues and moods, with varying effects. Aesthetic enjoyment of any of the fine arts was, in its highest stage, likened to the attainment of the mystical state of bliss, which itself was compared to the experience of oneness achieved during perfect sexual union. The great Hindu philosopher Abhinavagupta defined the highest type of aesthetic enjoyment as:

A feeling of expansiveness, a tendency to sublime manifestations, the experience of Truth-essence, delight in giving form and expression to one's innermost experience, of the nature of pure Joy and Bliss.

Of great importance in the Hindu appreciation of the arts is the concept of *Rasa* or "taste-essence," sometimes defined as "the reflex of sentiment." This term is used in reference to the taste of food, drama, poetry, music, most fine art and medicine. The sage Bharata, who codified the arts of dance and drama, declared that the meaning of this word is "that which is capable of being tasted." It is also used to describe content of an art work or performance, and is linked to the sweet taste when describing art of an erotic sentiment.

The linking of sentiments in Hindu culture has undergone careful scrutiny. Another classical work on the art of dance, written by Dhananjaya in the tenth century A.D., states:

One sentiment, either the heroic or the erotic, is

to be made the principle sentiment. All other sentiments should be kept subordinate.

Bharata explains the linkages in his text of the second century A.D.:

The comic sentiment arises from the erotic, the pitiful from the furious, the marvelous from the heroic, the terrific from the disgusting.

The changing moods of women were used as inspirational themes by many medieval Indian erotic artists. The fifteenth-century Hindu poet Bhanudatta classified these moods in his erotic masterpiece *Rasa Manjari* and personified them as "heroines" (*Nayikas*) who soon became very popular subjects for painters. Some of these heroine subjects are a woman devoted to her husband, a woman suffering from separation from her husband or lover, a shy woman about to meet her lover, a woman madly in love, a woman overcome with grief or anger at real or imagined neglect, a woman very conscious of her charms, a woman who feels she has her lover under a spell, a woman much frustrated, a woman upset at detecting the infidelity of her lover, a woman disappointed at the failure of her lover to keep his appointment with her, an exceedingly jealous woman, a woman in erotic expectancy, a woman dressed up in all her finery and in a mood to flaunt her beauty, a woman satiated by love's passion, and so forth.

A particular kind of Indian miniature paintings known as *Raga Mala* or "Rosary of Musical Modes" emerged between the sixteenth and eighteenth centuries. These paintings were inspired by *Nayika* or heroine themes and sought to express musical modes in visual form. They were organized like rich Hindu families, with each of the thirty-six *Ragas* having five or six "wives or mistresses" (*Raginis*), several sons (*Ragaputras*), daughters (*Ragaputris*) and so forth. Most of these paintings are of a subtle erotic type, showing the ecstasy of love, the pain of separation or other strongly emotional themes of love. The love heroes and heroines (*Nayakas* and *Nayikas*,

respectively) were like actors in a drama, aided by a suitably designed stage set, a backdrop and props. Everything would be carefully colored according to the required sentiment to be expressed. Erotic miniature paintings depicting love postures were often directly derived from *Raga Mala* paintings, which in turn were inspired by epic and romantic poetry, drama, dance or musical compositions.

The intimate relationship of the fine arts of music, drama, dance, painting, and the art of love itself, cannot be overstated. The traditional "language of signs," as outlined in the *Kama Sutra* and other erotic texts, in which precise choice and placement of flowers and fruits, touching or exposing specific parts of the body, selection of particular types and colors of clothing, flower garlands, spices and food preparations, different presentations of betel nuts and other condiments, was used to convey exact messages, usually of an erotic nature. For example, touching the chest means deep-seated love, touching the hair signifies passion, a red flower garland or red item of clothing communicates the desire for immediate lovemaking, whereas a yellow garment signifies separation or rejection. Color, facial expressions, bodily poses, hand gestures, choice of clothing and ornaments, indications of seasons, time of day, visual puns and the inclusion of highly suggestive symbolic objects are all very much part of the overall ingredients and composition of classical Indian paintings of an erotic type.

In Hindu culture erotic paintings often played an important role in the life of a person of means. A collection of fine erotic paintings could be used to instruct the ignorant in the arts of love, to help break the ground in a new relationship, to suggest subtle refinements of sexual behavior, to guide lovers to a higher aesthetic appreciation of intimacy, to stimulate fantasy, or just to entertain. A twelfth-century text, *Naisadhacharita* of Sri Harsha, gives a vivid description of a royal palace decorated with erotic art:

In the inner apartment there were images of Rati and Kama, the goddess and god of love, in union together. On the walls there were paintings of love dalliances and erotic sculptures illustrating mythic themes.

All such settings were carefully organized to stimulate the erotic sentiment in an aesthetically pleasing and highly refined way.

Illustrated erotic manuals or "love books," were given as gifts to the bride and groom at the traditional Hindu marriage ceremony. Erotic poetry or quotations from classical erotic literature would often be inscribed on these paintings, or on opposite pages in a book. The *Ananga Ranga*, a Hindu text on the art of love, written by Kalyanamalla in the fifteenth century, describes the way erotic paintings could be used to elevate the setting for a love tryst, and specifically mentions books containing illustrations of love postures:

Decorate the beautiful walls of the love-chamber with pictures and other objects upon which the eyes may dwell with delight. Scatter some musical instruments and refreshments, rosewater, essences, fans and books containing amorous songs and illustrations of love postures.

Erotic Miniature Paintings from India and Nepal

Erotic paintings have an ancient tradition in the Hindu art of love, serving to delight the eye, stimulate the senses, and convey important cultural, sexological, iconographic, and metaphysical information. Sequences of love postures are the principal theme, though the personages, facial expressions, color combinations, and symbolic content are all very significant and can be precisely interpreted. The overall effect of these fine paintings is to uplift the human spirit and bring it into harmony with nature through the power of the erotic sentiment.

The following full color reproductions of a selection of Hindu erotic paintings created between the early eighteenth and early twentieth century are representative of several different regional styles. The fifty-three paintings from India, done with natural mineral pigments on paper, are all true miniatures, best viewed close up. Included among these are fine miniatures from the Deccan, Bengal, Luchnow and Rajasthan, as well as an exquisite series of dated paintings from Jodhpur and several unusual examples in the East India Company style, a style which evolved during the nineteenth century as native artists absorbed European techniques. Some of these paintings were for sale to Europeans living in India.

The thirteen paintings from Nepal, done in Kathmandu around 1830 represent Hindu culture, which entered Nepal at an early period, and maintained its influence even during times when certain Nepali kings embraced the Buddhist faith. The postures, mystic gestures and other details illustrate a deep involvement with Tantric ritual. They are painted in a style derived from the famous Sirohi school, which evolved in Rajasthan, India. The paintings are much larger than the normal miniature, and can easily be viewed from across the room.

Painted with mineral colors on card, these paintings are the best examples from an extensive series depicting various oriental rulers in sexual union with favorites. The idea that rulers of nations could influence the destiny of a country by virtue of their proficiency in love techniques is very much a part of pagan culture, and there can be no doubt that these portrayals were created in the belief that they might serve such a function.

Over the centuries Indian artists developed a technology which enabled them to prepare lasting colors, fine hand-made paper and excellent brushes. Deep blue was made from finely ground lapis lazuli; red from cinnabar, iron oxide, or ochers; yellow from arsenic sulphide; and greens from malachite or copper salts. Papers were made from cotton fibers, hemp, bark, and bamboo, and were finely surfaced by polishing. Brushes were made from squirrel tails. Real gold and silver leaf were often used as embellishments.

All the paintings reproduced here were objects of study during our research for the publication *Sexual Secrets: The Alchemy of Ecstasy* (New York: Destiny Books, 1979). Our initial focus at that time was to discover accurate oriental renderings of the numerous lovemaking positions as described in the *Kama Sutra*, the *Ananga Ranga* and Tantric and Taoist Texts. We did succeed in finding many good examples to use as a basis for line illustrations in *Sexual Secrets*, and in the process uncovered a wealth of truly fine paintings which we felt should be published. A selection of these original paintings were published in full color as *The Pillow Book: The Erotic Sentiment and the Paintings of India, Nepal, China & Japan* (New York: Destiny Books, 1981). Although *The Pillow Book* is now out of print, interest in the material continues. This present volume, which contains additional material on India and Nepal, is the response to that interest.

Many of the illustrations are renderings of couples in love positions exactly as described in the classical texts. Some are elaborate and difficult Tantric love postures, used for controlling or channeling sexual energy, several depict polygamous situations, and others are fanciful groupings of couples made into a design. Tantric love postures, yogic gestures, symbolic color combinations, and the presence of ritual items all commonly occur in Indian erotic paintings, up to the present time, and are particularly frequent in examples created under royal patronage. Obvi-

ously such paintings were to be understood on several different levels, depending on the degree of familiarity with the esoteric content.

Ordinary couples, aristocrats, princes, and kings are all represented here in sexual union. As with most Indian and Nepali miniature painting, there is very little use of spacial perspective. In most instances the emphasis is placed on the couple, placed against a backdrop evocative of the sentiment, season or time of day. Various props are added, and these generally have symbolic meaning.

Particular care is taken with the treatment of the eyes, which are shown slightly overlarge. The facial expressions are mostly serene or sweet, as an indication of the erotic sentiment. Most of the paintings successfully convey an atmosphere of intimacy by the subtle blending of color tones and by the masterful use of form. The celebration of love as an art form is well represented in this group of paintings.

Many of the paintings have a jewel-like quality. In some the mood is serious while in others it is playful. The exotic combinations of vivid colors with pastel-like subtle tones help create a sentiment of eroticism which is accented by the actions of the main figures. This is not pornographic art but rather the celebration of the senses in all their glory. These paintings were created to be enjoyed, as lasting expressions of love itself. Here is an ancient art form that is truly a celebration of the creative erotic sentiment and the urge to ecstasy.

Nik Douglas

THE EROTIC SENTIMENT
In the Paintings of India and Nepal

In this rare and beautiful painting a Nepalese king is depicted in the role of Vishnu, the Hindu Lord of Preservation and Ruler over the erotic sentiment. His consort is shown as Lakshmi, goddess of prosperity and auspiciousness. This regal couple are in seated union upon a high throne supported by snow lions and elephants; a canopy of snakes rears up to protect them. Beyond, a pale full moon hangs in the dark night sky and illuminates the garden. The painting is inscribed Siddhi Narayan, meaning "The magical power of Vishnu."

A bearded man wearing a turban makes love to a reclining naked lady. Both wear jewels and garlands, perhaps indicating that they have just been married. This is a posture ideally suited for prolonged lovemaking. The red flowers on the carpet upon which they lie, and the red curtain draped and tied, suggest passion in the process of being fulfilled.

A regal couple are seated on an elaborate four-poster, canopied bed against a bright red background, signifying passion. They are in a Tantric posture used for channeling sexual energy upwards, so as to vitalize and uplift their spirits. The lavish setting and intense action of the composition help to create an atmosphere of mystic sensuality.

This interior scene depicts a dark-skinned Indian man uniting with a fair Indian woman with hennaed hands and feet. They are performing the Equal Peaks position of the Moon Elixir Tantra, devised to allow sustained rocking movements conducive to achieving ecstasy.

A moustached man wearing a flat hat and ornate jacket kneels and leans forward intensely as he makes love to a woman reclining on a carpet and supported by cushions. This may represent union between a merchant and a courtesan. They make love in the "Bow Position" as described in the Kama Sutra. The exploding star-like motifs on the carpet are used to dramatize the intensity of passion.

19

Maharaja Rajdullah Bahadur is shown in this detail from a Nepalese painting. He is seen kneeling on a throne while uniting with a favorite concubine and smoking a hookah. Together they are performing the Widely Open posture described in the Kama Sutra. The complementary colors of red and green and blue and orange provide a vibrant contrast to the white robes and pale complexions of the couple.

This Nepalese painting depicts Nadir Shah—the great Persian ruler who sacked Delhi and captured the Peacock Throne—seated in union with a beautiful woman whose hands and feet are red with henna. Perhaps he is "conquering Delhi" (symbolized by his Indian partner), since he sits on the Peacock Throne and holds a sword in his right hand. His consort seems to be an adept of sexual yoga, for she holds her legs with her hands in a way designed to harness the outward flow of sexual energy.

How delicious an instrument is woman, when artfully played upon; how capable is she of producing the most exquisite harmonies, of executing the most complicated variations of love, and of giving the most Divine of erotic pleasures.

Ananga Ranga

This exquisite Nepalese painting depicts a royal couple in the Mounted Yantra posture of the Moon Elixir Tantra. The mood is filled with romance as the lovers unite under the moon and stars. The combination of textures and designs contrasts beautifully with the colors and tones of the composition and helps convey a sentiment of sweetness and passion.

This fine painting shows a richly dressed Maharaja seated on the terrace of his palace while he playfully fondles his beautiful consort; the lotus crown on his head suggests a high level of spiritual attainment. As he leans against sumptuous cushions, his partner clasps her arms around his neck and gazes at his face adoringly. The fresh, clean mineral colors of this composition create a mood of natural harmony.

A Maharaja unites with two consorts on the terrace of a palace. Resting on brightly colored cushions, the bodies of the two women conjoin as their lover's Lingam enters each Yoni in turn. Together they perform the United Position, described in the Kama Sutra. To one side a red flame burns majestically in a lamp, symbolizing the spiritual quality of this union free from jealousy.

In this detail from a miniature painting, a noble couple unite in the standing position known as *Three Steps of Vishnu*.

This detail from a superb miniature painting depicts a Maharaja in seated union with his beautiful consort. They make love in a version of the All-Around position, described in the Ananga Ranga. As the man supports himself with cushions, his partner clasps him around the neck and looks up at him adoringly. Ritual items and refreshments are scattered in the foreground.

In this watercolor from an unusual series of miniatures in the European style of the East India Company school, a courtesan or lady musician is shown seated in union upon a reclining man, probably of the merchant class. She is performing a variation of the position "Bee Buzzing over Man" as described in the Ananga Ranga, and plays a stringed instrument as she performs for her client. Usually, Indian subjects are painted in an Indian style rather than the European style employed here.

This unusual Nepalese painting depicts a great Mongolian ruler reclining on a temple terrace while his beautiful consort makes love to him in the Tantric posture known as *Bee Buzzing over Man*. Both wear Mongolian felt boots and exquisite ornaments, and the man rests on fine cushions. To one side the entrance of a temple is embellished with the sacred monogram known as *Auspicious Seven*, composed of seed-syllables of the vital centers and elements, with a scepter motif and the sacred syllable OM overhead, inscribed in Tibetan characters.

This sensitive Nepalese painting depicts the Persian ruler Muhammad Shah seated in union upon a throne placed upon the terrace of a palace. A beautiful woman perches daintily upon his massive thigh, smiling as she playfully fondles his chin with her hennaed right hand. Despite the Shah's opulence, a sweet sentiment pervades, conveyed through the charming use of color, the flower gardens beyond, and the childlike sensuality of his delightful consort.

This exquisite detail from a Nepalese painting depicts Badshah Jehangir and Begum Nur Jahan seated in union upon the Peacock Throne which rests on the terrace of a palace. As these famous lovers unite their bodies in the Gaining-Restraining posture of the Ananga Ranga, they look lovingly into each other's eyes. The rich colors and fine details give a regal air to this magnificent composition.

This unusual Nepalese painting shows a noble warrior making love to his consort on the terrace of a palace. They have united their bodies in a Tantric pose; their feet are joined and their hands are placed on their knees to create a closed energy circuit between them. This posture is said to have derived from the lovemaking of butterflies.

A man wearing a soldier's uniform stands on a palace terrace and makes love to a noblewoman who supports herself on a high podium and cushions. The woman's almond-shaped eyes gaze upward as her partner takes the active role. The delightful combination of yellow, orange, and cream contrasts exquisitely with the cool silver and blue of the sky behind.

An Indian Ruler and his queen are shown making love in a position known as a Bandha or "lock," used to control the outward flow of sexual energy. The feet and hands of the woman are red with henna, indicating that she has been prepared for this Tantric practice. The couple gaze upward to the sky, as if recalling their Divine Origin. Ritual items and refreshments are shown in the foreground.

This delicately toned painting depicts a prince or Maharaja in Tantric union with a queen or favorite concubine. This posture is a variation of the "Turning Position" described in the Kama Sutra and is very similar to that referred to as "Reverse Monkey" in the Ananga Ranga. Very little movement is possible in this position, which is recommended for prolonged lovemaking leading to ecstasy.

A noble couple unite upon the terrace of a palace. They have formed their bodies into a mystic love posture, linking hands and raising up their legs to create an upliftment of sexual energy. An aureole of celestial color is visible behind the man's head, symbolizing the spiritual fruit of such practices.

Though a woman is naturally reserved and keeps her feelings concealed,
yet when she gets on top of a man she should show all her love and
desire.

Kama Sutra

A noblewoman takes the active role in performing the first stage of the Swing posture, described in the
Kama Sutra. The man cups his partner's face in his hand, as if to seal her mouth, while she holds up a
golden wine cup out of his reach.

This detail from the same series as the previous example depicts a woman lying back upon a red cushion while her noble lover unites with her in a version of the All-Encompassing position of the Ananga Ranga.

In this detail from a Nepalese painting, a noble couple are depicted in union upon a decorated red carpet. The woman's head rests on a pillow as she raises her legs and performs the Opening and Blossoming position described in the Ananga Ranga. The combination of intense red and pale, cool hues conveys a mood of ardor tempered by calm detachment.

From the same series of Nepalese paintings comes this exquisite detail of a royal couple making love with the woman in the superior role. Together this couple perform the Pair of Tongs posture, described in the Ananga Ranga. The sacred seed-syllable OM can be seen in the background. The mood expressed by this painting is a combination of sensuality and sensitivity.

A noble couple make love in a covered pavilion as a maidservant waits in attendance. They are performing a variation of the Supported Position of the Kama Sutra. Storm clouds loom in the sky and contrast with the fresh, bright colors of the main composition.

Here a noble couple perform a highly complex love posture, supporting themselves on cushions which rest upon an ornate carpet. As they unite in a kind of lover's knot, the man gazes intensely at his consort and artfully fondles her breast with his foot. The composition of this painting conveys a mood of controlled dynamism and balance.

It is the duty of the man to consider the tastes of woman and to be tough or tender, according to his beloved's wishes.

Koka Shastra

A noble couple unite in a red room adjoining a walled terrace. As the man holds his Lingam and places it within the Yoni of his beloved, she leans back over a white bed and playfully twirls his moustache with her hennaed fingers. A female musician kneels on the terrace outside, providing sweet melodies to accompany the movements of love.

This detail shows a noble couple making love in the unusual Spinning Top posture, described in the Kama Sutra. As the Maharaja reclines, his consort takes up this acrobatic position over him; a maidservant rocks the bed while handing her mistress a cup of wine.

Here a noble couple are captured in the midst of sexual play upon twin swings. They press the soles of their feet together, creating love rhythms as the swings move back and forth. Such ingenious sexual aids were not uncommon in the Orient, serving to heighten erotic fantasy and joyful spontaneity.

A peacock struts on a wall above a noble couple seated in union on the terrace of a palace. The lovers rock backward and forward, placing their hands in mystic gestures devised to channel sexual energy.

In this watercolor miniature from an unusual European style series from the East India Company school, a young man wearing a red jacket and turban is depicted in union with a lady in a variation of the "Turning Position" as described in the Kama Sutra. He kneels on his right knee and raises his left knee as he takes the woman from behind. His partner looks upward in abandonment.

This intimate view inside a palace shows a Hindu Maharaja kneeling upon a bed and entering his consort's body as she raises her legs in the classic love posture known as Alternate Yawning. The couple gaze intently into each other's eyes while a female attendant moves a fly-whisk over them and aids their love movements by rocking the bed. The use of the complementary colors of lilac and yellow ocher, red and green, instills a mood of harmony and psychic upliftment.

When both are locked in the embrace of love,
There is no separateness, no "good" or "bad";
All thoughts vanish
With the onslaught of pure passion.
Kuttni Mahatmyam

An Indian couple are seated indoors in the Lotus Position of the Ananga Ranga. The man's face carries an impassive expression as he concentrates on retention; the woman's long braid falls down her back like a thin black snake. The skin tones contrast well with the palette used in the rest of the composition.

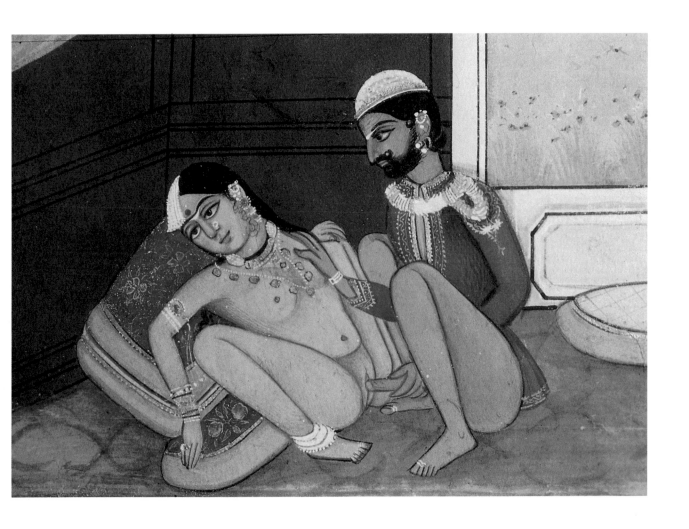

In this detail an Indian couple unite within the confines of a house. The man squats and holds his Lingam to his partner's Yoni as she leans back on crimson cushions. The woman's naked body is covered with fine jewelry and her forehead bears a red mark. This couple are performing a version of the classic Indrani posture of the Kama Sutra.

A noble couple makes love on a palace terrace, a dark stormy sky overhead. The man kneels on one knee and aims an arrow at a white crane flying overhead; a sword and shield lie discarded at his feet. A naked consort sits in union upon him, her head turned toward his target. The bow and arrow bring to mind Kama Deva, the Hindu love god who, like Cupid, shoots "arrows of desire."

A noble couple are shown making love on an exotic canopied bed located on a palace terrace underneath a crescent moon; stars shine in the lilac sky above. The lovers are performing a variation of the Tantric posture known as Fixing a Nail, described in the Kama Sutra.

An oval vignette frames a regal couple who make love on an ornate carpet and are supported by cushions. They are within a palace setting and are in an early phase of the "Bird Position" as described in the Ananga Ranga. The swirling clouds visible in the sky behind the couple evoke the sentiment of urgent passion.

A Hindu Maharaja is seated on a palace terrace. His beautiful consort performs oral love as he reclines against a large cushion; flowers burst into bloom in the background. This detail is from a particularly fine Indian painting.

In this detail a noble couple are shown seated in Tantric union upon a white bed within a red room. The couple embrace and make love in a version of the *Thigh-Rubbing* posture of the *Moon Elixir Tantra*. As the man clasps his partner's leg, she holds up a cup of wine.

Another seated love posture is shown in this detail from the same series as the previous example. The couple perform the Gaining-Restraining position described in the Ananga Ranga and rock their bodies back and forth underneath a blue and red canopy.

The wife is half the man, his priceless friend;
Of pleasure, virtue, wealth, his constant source;
A help throughout his earthly years;
Through life unchanging, even beyond its end.
                                        Mahabharata

Day passes into night in this exquisite Nepalese painting of a noble couple standing in erotic union on a palace terrace. The woman holds back her raven tresses as her lover clasps her diaphanous robe in one hand and cups her left breast with the other hand. With her delicate skin and sensuous pose, the royal consort seems like a carved statue coming to life. White birds and pink and blue flowers bedeck the tree branches as the sun sets in a rosy shimmer. The mood is enchanting, evoking the sentiment of sensual love.

The ecstatic union of a regal couple is beautifully portrayed in this detail. A Maharaja squats over his consort, penetrating her as she lies back on a bed placed on an outside terrace. As the man moves his "Scepter" within his partner's "Lotus," he gazes intensely into her eyes and performs the Bird Position described in the Ananga Ranga. This is perhaps a Tantric rite performed in the dead of night.

This fine watercolor depicts a man reclining on a couch while his consort squats upon him in the Tantric love posture known as *Bee Buzzing over Man*, described in the *Ananga Ranga*. The woman holds a lyre and makes sweet music while loving her enraptured partner.

This lyrical watercolor depicts a nobleman reclining in the arms of his beautiful consort, who shares an ornate cushioned couch with him. The parrot perched on the pillow symbolizes Mohini the Temptress. The flowing spontaneity of line and color shows a real mastery of technique.

A noble couple are entwined upon a love seat while a parrot perches nearby. As the woman holds a lotus bud, symbolic of spiritual passion, she looks lovingly at her partner, who fondles her breast. The mood of this flowing composition is joyous.

A couple make love upon a couch. He leans over his partner, allowing his Lingam to enter her Yoni;
she encourages him and holds a lotus in her right hand. A feeling of ardor is lyrically conveyed through
the free yet economic use of line and tone.

A noble couple are shown in the first stage of the Indrani posture, as described in the Kama Sutra. The woman leans back, as her lover enters her Yoni. A small gold box, probably for betel nut, is shown at one side. The fine line and light color wash create an atmosphere of reserved refinement.

A nobleman kneels formally as he makes love to his beautiful consort in a variation of the classical Turning Posture. As the woman turns around to face him, she fans him from behind. The exquisite gold and red details contrast greatly with the light color wash of the composition.

A noble couple make love on a rug surrounded by lotus motifs, with refreshments placed close by. They perform the Variegated posture of the Moon Elixir Tantra, supporting their bodies on a pink cushion. The pastel colors and sensitive treatment of the faces help create a mystic mood.

A Hindu Maharaja kneels in full regalia in erotic union with his consort on a palace terrace. This noble couple are performing a version of the classical Indrani posture. The woman's hands and feet are ritually hennaed. She is exquisitely adorned and as she leans back upon cushions her vermilion skirt opens like a fan, contrasting with the white robes of the ruler. In the foreground are displayed weapons, ritual items, and refreshments; a bird cage and a hookah are shown behind. Beyond, on the horizon, greens melt into blue; nature becomes celestial.

This beautiful Nepalese painting shows a Maharaja and his queen tenderly making love on a carpet placed upon a palace terrace. Both are kneeling, with arms around each other in a variation of the esoteric Pleasure-Evoking posture of the Moon Elixir Tantra. As the couple exchange loving gazes, drinking in each other's spiritual essence, their gentle mood is echoed in the pink cursive clouds floating in the blue sky above. The Maharaja's skin is soft pale pink, and his consort's flesh is like precious ivory.

A noble couple acrobatically make love on the terrace of a palace. The man arches his body like a bow and his consort balances on top of him, performing the Spinning Top position, described in the Kama Sutra. Refreshments and ritual items can be seen on the carpet about them, and trees laden with fruit and flowers are visible in the gardens.

Here a detail from a miniature painting shows a nobleman and his consort in union upon a white bed located within the courtyard of a palace. She crosses her legs and reclines against a cushion, so creating the Lotus-like posture described in the Kama Sutra. The brightly colored geometric shapes of the building contrast excitingly with the bold design of the couple's united bodies.

In another detail from the same series as the previous example a nobleman is shown seated in yogic posture upon a bed. His beautiful partner sits on top of his erect Lingam as they perform a version of the Tantric love position known as Splitting a Bamboo, described in the Kama Sutra. Effective use is made of the flat areas of subtle color, creating an intensely dynamic and erotic mood.

An exquisite detail of a miniature painting shows a Maharaja uniting with five consorts. Each woman plays an instrument, creating a "symphony of love" as their lord harmonizes with each of them simultaneously. Ritual items and refreshments grace the foreground, and lush gardens can be seen in the background. A sweet and lyrical sentiment pervades this scene of erotic harmony.

Having made a pillow of each other's arms,
And twining legs with legs,
With minds freed from doubt and shame,
We have not cooled the natural urges
Of our passionate longing.

Kuttni Mahatmyam

This detail from an exquisite miniature painting depicts a Maharaja uniting with two consorts supporting themselves on each other as his Lingam enters the Yoni of each in turn. In this unusual version of the United Position, both women turn toward the ruler, their eyes wide in expectancy. Flowers burst into bloom in the background, which is artfully set against silver.

71

A Maharaja reclines on a couch while engaging in a form of multiple lovemaking referred to in the *Kama Sutra* as the *Herd of Cows*. His principle consort takes the active role, squatting over the erect Lingam of her lord, while he stimulates the exposed Yonis of three other ladies. A fifth woman stands in attendance holding flowers.

This unusual miniature painting shows a mythological scene, created to attract good fortune through the power of sex. The winged "trick horse" is made up of naked copulating couples artfully entwined. In many Oriental cultures the power of sex is used on a symbolic level, in the belief that it helps attract good luck.

A Hindu Maharaja unites with his principle consort and two concubines. A sword and shield suggest that this ruler is of the warrior caste. The two lamps over the concubines symbolize that a spiritual rite is being portrayed. This depiction of multiple loving can also be interpreted as the union of the three main subtle nerve-channels of the Tantric tradition.

A Hindu Maharaja with a blue and gold halo about his head is shown riding a "trick horse" composed of many naked couples. He holds a rose in his left hand and raises it upward as he rides majestically across the courtyard of a palace. Undoubtedly this fine painting was created as a charm to ensure the prosperity of a ruler.

An oval vignette frames a pair of noble lovers who are seated in a version of the Gemini Position described in the Ananga Ranga. The man leans back on a large pink cushion, his Lingam slightly withdrawn from the Yoni, while his consort raises a cup of wine to his lips. The expanse of blue behind them adds an almost celestial quality to this exquisite composition.

This extraordinary composition depicts a Maharaja seated in a chariot created by seven naked women. On a symbolic level this scene portrays a ruler in the role of the sun god, who, according to traditional Hindu iconography, rides a chariot pulled by seven horses. The light and dark blue background contrasts with the rich gold and crimson of the Maharaja riding this unusual "chariot," probably composed of women from his harem.

This "trick horse" is composed of a number of couples in union. A Hindu queen is shown in the riding position, a wand of jasmine flowers in her hand. A woman raises her hennaed fingers to create the impression of animal ears. This rare painting must have been created for a Tantric rite of psychic protection.

This rare Nepalese painting shows a king in seated union with his beautiful consort. Two fishes, symbolizing the virile power of Vishnu, can be seen under him as he aims a "love arrow" at five women who are paying homage to him. This highly symbolic scene represents the ruler in his role of Kama Deva, the ever-virile god of love.

BIBLIOGRAPHY

Anand, Mulk Raj. *Kama Kala*. Geneva: Nagel, 1963.

Arbuthnot, F. F. and Richard F. Burton. *Ananga Ranga: Stage of the Bodiless One, the Hindu Art of Love.* New York: Medical Press, 1964.

Arbuthnot, F. F. and Richard F. Burton, *The Kama Sutra of Vatsyayana*. London: George Allen and Unwin, 1963.

Bhattacharyya, Narendra Nath. *History of Indian Erotic Literature*. New Delhi: Munshiram Manoharlal, 1975.

Bowie, Theodore, and Cornelia V. Christenson. *Studies in Erotic Art*. New York: Basic Books, 1970.

Chandra, Moti. *The World Of Courtesans*. New Delhi: Vikas Publishing, 1973.

Comfort, Alex. *The Koka Shastra, and Other Indian Writings on Love*. London: George Allen and Unwin, 1964.

Dallapiccola, A. L. *Princesses et Courtisanes A Travers Les Miniatures Indiennes*. Paris: Marco Polo, 1978.

Dallapiccola, A. L. *Ragamala*. Paris: Marco Polo, 1977.

Desai, Devangara. *Erotic Sculpture of India*. New Delhi: Tata McGraw Hill, 1975.

Douglas, Nik. *The Art of Love*. Beverly Hills: Kreitman Gallery, 1979.

Douglas, Nik, and Penny Slinger. *Sexual Secrets: The Alchemy of Ecstasy*. New York: Destiny Books, 1979.

Douglas, Nik, and Penny Slinger. *The Pillow Book: The Erotic Sentiment and the Paintings of India, Nepal, China and Japan*. New York: Destiny Books, 1981.

Ebeling, Klaus. *Ragamala Painting*. Basel: Ravi Kumar, 1973.

Fouchet, Max-Pol. *The Erotic Sculpture of India*. New York: Criterion Books, 1959.

Gerhard, Poul. *Pornography or Art?* Bishop's Stortford, England: Words and Pictures, 1971.

Gregersen, Edgar. *Sexual Practices: The Story of Human Sexuality*. London: Mitchell Beazley, 1982.

Heeramaneck, Alice. *Masterpieces of Indian Painting*. New York: Heeramaneck Publishing, 1984.

Kronhausen, Phyllis, and Eberhard Kronhausen. *The Complete Book of Erotic Art*. New York: Bell, 1978.

Kronhausen, Phyllis, and Eberhard Kronhausen. *Catalogue of the International Museum of Erotic Art*. San Francisco: National Sex Forum, 1973.

Lal, Kanwar. *The Cult of Desire: An Interpretation of Erotic Sculpture of India*. New York: University Books, 1967.

Lal, Kanwar. *Kanya and the Yogi*. New Delhi: Arts and Letters, 1970.

Lal, Kanwar. *Erotic Sculpture of Khajuraho*. New Delhi: Asia Press, 1970.

Mandel, G., and F. M. Ricci. *Tantra: Rites of Love*. New York: Rizzoli, 1979.

Mathers, E., and Powys. *Eastern Love*. London: John Rudker, 1951.

Meyer, Johann Jakob. *Sexual Life in Ancient India*. Varanasi, India: Motilal Banarsidass, 1971.

Mookerjee, Ajit. *Tantra Art*. Basel: Ravi Kumar, 1971.

Mookerjee, Ajit. *Tantra Asana*. Basel: Ravi Kumar, 1971.

Randhawa, Mohinder Singh, and John Kenneth Galbraith. *Indian Painting: The Scene, Themes and Legends*. New York: Houghton Mifflin, 1968.

Rawson, Philip. *Erotic Art of the East*. New York: Prometheus, 1968.

Rawson, Philip. *Tantra: Catalogue of an Exhibition at the Haywood Gallery*. London: Arts Council, 1971.

Rawson, Philip. *Tantra: The Indian Cult of Ecstasy*. London: Thames and Hudson, 1973.

Rawson, Philip. *Erotic Art of India*. London: Thames and Hudson, 1977.

Sen, R. K. *Aesthetic Enjoyment: Its Background in Philosophy and Medicine*. Calcutta: University of Calcutta, 1966.

Shukla, D. N. *Hindu Canons of Iconography*. Gorakhpur, India: Gorakhpur University Press, 1958.

Shukla, D. N. *Royal Palace and Royal Arts*. Lucknow, India: Vastuvanmaya, 1967.

Shukla, D. N. *Royal Arts*. Lucknow, India: Vastuvanmaya, 1967.

Smedt, Marc de. *The Kama Sutra: Erotic Figures in Indian Art*. New York: Crescent Books, 1980.

Smith, Bradley. *Erotic Art of the Masters*. La Jolla, California: Gemini-Smith, no date.

Thomas, P. *Kama Kalpa: The Hindu Ritual of Love*. Bombay: Taraporevala, 1959.

Tucci, Giuseppe. *Rati Lila: An Interpretation of the Tantric Imagery of the Temples of Nepal*. Geneva: Nagel, 1969.

Wilson, H. H. *The Theatre of the Hindus*. Calcutta: Susil Gupta, 1955.